To the memory of the real Papa and Mama of this story,
John Belton Harper and Margaret Mae Ashworth Harper, and to
their descendants, especially those of Mae Dean Harper Bley,
the child who never forgot the trip up the caprock— Jo Harper and Josephine Harper

For Robin, who's keen eyes see what I miss— Craig Spearing

Turtle
B O O K S

Prairie Dog Pioneers

Text copyright © 1998 by Jo & Josephine Harper
Illustrations copyright © 1998 by Craig Spearing

First Published in 1998 by Turtle Books

For information or permissions, address:
Turtle Books, 866 United Nations Plaza, Suite 525
New York, New York 10017

Cover and book design by Jessica Kirchoff Bowlby
Text of this book is set in Goudy Old Style Roman
Illustrations are from cut linoleum block prints printed on Rives BFK acid-free paper,
which were then colored with a base of watercolors, followed by Prisma colored pencil highlighting.
The traditional American folksong—'Home on the Range'—(page 46) was set as a musical score by Denise Hoff/MediaLynx, Inc.
First Edition
Smyth sewn, cambric reinforced binding, printed on 80# Evergreen matte natural, acid-free paper
Printed and bound in the United States of America

10 9 8 7 6 5 4 3 2 1

Library of Congress Cataloging-in-Publication Data
Harper, Jo. Prairie Dog Pioneers / Jo & Josephine Harper ; illustrated by Craig Spearing.   p.   cm.
Summary: Because Mae Dean misinterprets her father's actions while journeying to their new home
on the Texas prairie, she begins to feel that he doesn't care for her anymore.
ISBN 1-890515-10-8 (hardcover : alk. paper)
[1. Frontier and pioneer life—Texas—Fiction. 2. Fathers and daughters—Fiction.
3. Moving, Household—Fiction. 4. Texas—Fiction.]
I. Harper, Josephine, 1953-   . II. Spearing, Craig, ill. III. Title.
PZ7.H23135Pr 1998 [E]—dc21 98-9678 CIP AC

Distributed by Publishers Group West

ISBN 1-890515-10-8

Prairie Dog Pioneers

Jo & Josephine Harper

illustrated by Craig Spearing

Turtle Books
NEW YORK

The Panhandle

TEXAS

❧ Authors' Prologue ❧

The Panhandle of Texas remained empty until almost the end of the 19th century. The area was not vast when compared to the size of the rest of the state, but it was formidable. Fierce rains came, but the sun and wind whisked the moisture away and periods of drought were long. Even the Comanche and buffalos could not live on that waterless plain. Rather, they swept across it, persistent and transient as the wind.

In 1874, buffalo hunters—greedy for the animals' hides—swept into Texas and waited for the annual migration of the American bison onto the Southern range. Texans went to the legislature in Austin and demanded that the hunters be stopped, but General Sheridan argued against them and won. The buffalos were hunted until the great herds were gone.

The end of the buffalo herds spelled the end of Comanche power. In 1875, Chief Quanah Parker surrendered and the plains were opened. Even then, they could not be settled—not until land-hungry farmers found water deep underground. And not until they had windmills light enough to carry in wagons but strong enough to withstand high-plains winds. Only then could they conquer that land, and they did—in record time.

Our own ancestors, John Belton Harper and Margaret Mae Ashworth Harper, were among the first to settle on the Texas side of the Red River. John Belton, like his Scottish forebears who were driven from their holdings, believed that only by owning land could a man be secure. When he died, he left a farm to each of his and Margaret Mae's nine children.

Their daughter, Mae Dean, was only four years old when the family went up the caprock, but she never forgot the sight of the water rushing down like a waterfall. She never forgot the darkness under the slicker or the sound of the rain beating on it. We are grateful that she told the story; that her grandson, Carl Bley, filmed her telling it; and that we now have an opportunity to share it with you, our gentle readers.

—JO AND JOSEPHINE HARPER

"Papa! Papa! You're home!" Mae Dean jumped from her swing and ran down the path. She felt herself lifted high and wrapped in a big warm hug. She loved the way Papa smelled—like hay and horses and leather.

"How's my blue-eyed girl?" he asked. Mae Dean was the only one in the family who looked like Papa, and she was glad. He was her hero.

Mama came and kissed Papa.

"I did it, Margaret Mae. I bought the land," Papa said. Mae Dean's older brothers—Jim, Hollis, Reed, Franklin, and Leo—all came running.

"Boys, we have our own land now and nobody can ever chase us off. I've already put down a windmill. Get ready to move!"

Move? Mae Dean's happiness dried up like water on parched ground.

Mama looked like she was trying to be brave, but Reed laughed. "Prairie dog pioneers, that's what we'll be," he said.

Reed was always making jokes, but Mae Dean didn't think this joke was funny. Prairie dogs were like squirrels only they lived under ground. "Prairie dog pioneers" didn't make sense.

The next afternoon, Mae Dean sat in her shady swing. The grass brushed against her feet and she could smell the honeysuckle and Mama's roses.

How could they leave their friends and their house with the colored glass in the front door? What about Mama's flowers? Mae Dean knew Mama didn't want to go either.

Papa just didn't understand.

That week, Papa sold their house and their furniture. He sold their buggy and the high stepping pony that pulled it. Then he bought big, heavy horses and a covered wagon. Their friends—the Mathis and the Barton families—bought covered wagons, too. They all were going to travel together.

In the evenings, after supper, Mae Dean sat in Papa's lap. He and her oldest brother, Jim, talked about cattle and crops.

"It's rich land," Papa would say. "Flat and clean." Mae Dean wanted to say, Don't make me move! But she didn't. She couldn't say that to Papa.

Early one morning before the sun was up, they left their home in Estelline. Papa drove the wagon and Mama sat in the back. Mae Dean and her youngest brother, Leo, nestled on quilts close to Mama. Her older middle brothers—Hollis, Franklin, and Reed—rode their ponies. And way back behind their family friends—the Mathises and the Bartons—Mae Dean's tall and oldest brother, Jim, drove a wagon loaded with lumber and supplies. They rode for hours.

"Papa, let's stop and eat," Mae Dean called up to her father.

But Papa shook his head. "Look at those thunderheads. We have to get up the caprock before it rains."

But soon rain began falling in great drops. Papa was frowning.

They came to a place where the ground rose in front of them like a cliff. They had reached the base of the caprock. Mr. Mathis signaled to Papa to stop. Mae Dean heard the men talking.

Papa said, "We have to push on up the caprock. This rain could turn into a flash flood."

Mr. Mathis shouted, "We can't get the wagons up that cliff! We have to wait for the rain to stop."

Papa shouted back over the wind and rain, "My horses are strong. I'm going up."

Papa got back in the wagon and cracked his whip. The wagon moved forward. Papa cracked the whip again and again. Mae Dean covered her face. She couldn't stand for Papa to hurt the horses.

"He's not hitting them," Mama said in Mae Dean's ear. "He's cracking the whip close to their heads so they can hear over the thunder. The sound of the whip tells them to go faster."

Water rushed down the cliff, and the horses rushed to meet it.

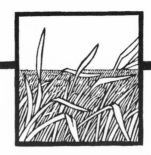

Through the rain, Mae Dean saw Mr. Mathis ride close to their wagon.

"Ashworth, are you crazy?" he shouted. "That wagon will turn over. You'll kill them all."

Papa stood up and cracked the whip. The wagon lurched forward.

Mae Dean felt hot. Her heart beat faster than the rain. How could Papa do this?

Mr. Mathis shouted, "Dean Ashworth, you're not going to kill this little one!" Then he leaned toward the wagon.

Suddenly, Mae Dean felt herself swooped up. Cold rain hit her; then everything was dark and dry. She was under Mr. Mathis' slicker.

The horse slipped, then steadied. Mae Dean could tell that they were climbing. They must be going up the caprock.

Mr. Mathis' strong arm held her. He was making sure she was safe. Papa should have done that.

The rain was loud against the slicker. Mae Dean felt like crying.

Mae Dean heard Papa's voice. "Mathis, I told you I could make it to the top. Now we can double-team the other wagons up."

Mr. Mathis lifted his slicker and gently put Mae Dean in Mama's arms. Mama's face was wet with rain; for a moment, Mae Dean thought the raindrops were tears. She and Mama watched the other wagons lurch up to join them.

When the rain stopped, the air was fresh and sweet. A rainbow arched across the heavens, and the prairie stretched before them.

There was nothing but grass and sky in any direction. No houses. No fences. No trees. No rivers. No hills. The green-brown of the prairie grass went on and on until it met the sky. Clouds hung like mountains in the distance.

"You can see clear to the end of the world up here," Mr. Barton said.

"Further," said Mrs. Barton. "You can see to the end of forever!"

Mae Dean stayed close to Mama. When Papa came near, she turned away.

The three fathers and their sons rubbed the horses down and fed them. Then the children played tag and turned cartwheels. They laughed when they landed in puddles.

Mae Dean didn't play, and she didn't laugh. She just wanted to sit in her swing. She wanted to go back home to Estelline.

Jim took firewood from the supply wagon and built a campfire. Mama, Mrs. Mathis, and Mrs. Barton cooked corn and bacon. They fried bread and opened two big jars of jelly.

"Here's a treat to celebrate getting up the caprock safely," Mama said.

"I'm not hungry," Mae Dean answered.

After supper, Papa got out his mandolin. "I have a new song I'd like to teach you. I think it is just right for us. It's called "Home on the Range."

Papa began to sing, "Oh, give me a home where the buffalo roam...."

Soon others joined in. "Home, home on the range, where the deer and the antelope play...."

Mae Dean hated that song because she didn't want the range to be her home. But everyone else loved it. Someone was still singing when Mae Dean lay down for the night. She snuggled close to Mama and covered her ears.

As they crossed the prairie, their wagon wheels left narrow tracks on the grass behind them, and the wind blew in their faces.

On the seventh day, Papa pointed. "Look!" he said. "That's our place!"

Mae Dean looked hard. She could barely make out one lonely shape against the sky. As they got closer, she saw that the shape was a windmill.

Finally they reached it. Everyone scrambled out of the wagons and gathered around the water barrel.

"We made it!"

"We're here!"

They drank cold windmill water, and they watered the stock. They splashed their windburnt faces.

"This is our new home," Papa told Mae Dean.

There was no tree for a swing. There wasn't even a house. Mae Dean's lip trembled.

"Now we have to dig a house like the prairie dogs do," Reed said with a laugh.

The sun was hot. Mae Dean and Mama got under the wagon for shade while the men began to build a dugout.

Papa, Mr. Mathis, and Mr. Barton cut sod into big squares and stacked them to one side. All the boys helped. They spaded out dirt and made a big hole, as deep as Papa was tall. The sides were straight and the corners were sharp.

Papa and the men took the sod squares and lined them along the edges of the hole, into short walls. With the lumber they had brought, they made a door on the south side, away from the winter winds. And they made a sloped roof of boards and poles covered with brush, dirt, and sod. They worked together for almost a week.

When the dugout was finished, Mama lighted a kerosene lamp and took Mae Dean down inside. The air smelled damp and musty. Dirt fell from the roof.

Papa joined them. He put his arm around Mama's shoulders. He cupped Mae Dean's chin in his hand.

"Things will get better," he said. "We'll make this dugout a home. You'll see. Someday, we'll build another house.

Mae Dean turned her face away.

Papa announced, "I'm going to leave now. I have to get supplies and then help the Bartons and the Mathises build dugouts on their land," Papa said.

Mae Dean ran up the sod steps, away from Papa. He was going to leave them alone in a little hole on this big prairie.

Mama said, "Papa will be back in just two weeks." She acted like that was only a little while, but it seemed like a long time to Mae Dean.

They put in the garden while Papa was gone. As they worked, they sang to keep up their spirits. Mae Dean joined in except when they sang Papa's new song, "Home on the Range." Then she pressed her lips together hard.

One day Mae Dean found a sandy spot on the prairie. The sandy land lay lower than the grassland. It was a little sheltered from the wind. She sat down, took her shoes off, and wiggled her toes. The warm sand felt smooth to her feet.

A prairie dog sat not far away. His little back was straight, and he fixed his eyes on her. She heard excited chattering. Nearby was a whole town of prairie dogs. "We Ashworths are just like you," she said. "I didn't want to live in the ground and be a prairie dog pioneer, but I am one."

Mae Dean dug her fingers into the sand. It was crusty at the top but soft underneath. She made little sand houses along a street. Each house had a yard and some tall grass clumps for trees. She made a little swing for one house. The sky was red with sunset when Mae Dean stopped.

Mama was outside cooking supper when Mae Dean got home. Every evening after they ate, Mama put her ear to the ground and listened. This time she said, "Papa is coming!"

Mae Dean and Jim put their ears to the ground. Mae Dean felt a pulse, then a pause, a pulse, then a pause.

Then Reed put his ear to the ground. "I hear horses!" he shouted.

Suddenly, the northern sky grew black. Lightning flashed, and in a few moments, a great clap of thunder followed. Big drops of rain began to fall. They hurried into the dugout. Mama lighted their covered lantern, and Jim stuck it outside on a stick so Papa could find them.

Mae Dean waited with her arms around her legs and her chin on her knees. It seemed like a long time.

"Ho! I'm home!" At last the call rang out above the noise of the rain. Jim pushed the dugout door and Papa came in with the wind.

He was dripping wet. "I made it!" he said. He smiled at them all. Mae Dean did not smile back.

Early in the morning, while everyone was still sleeping, Mae Dean slipped outside.

The wind and rain had stopped. The morning was pale and still. Mae Dean tore across the prairie. She had to see about her town.

The houses she had built the day before were washed away. Instead of the smooth sandy ground where she had dug and built, she saw only a pond of water. Across the way, a prairie dog called. Mae Dean sat down and cried.

A shadow fell in front of Mae Dean. She looked up to see who was there. It was Papa.

Mae Dean jumped to her feet. "Why did you bring us to live in this awful place? Yesterday I built a play-like town. Even a play-like town is better than no town at all. But now it's gone. All you care about is stupid old land. You don't care about me, not one bit."

Mae Dean had never spoken so rudely to anyone in her whole life, much less to Papa. She trembled. But she couldn't stop.

"Mr. Mathis cares more about me than you do. He kept me safe when we came up the caprock. You didn't even care if I got killed."

Papa bent over and picked Mae Dean up. He held her against his chest. He rocked gently from side to side. He smelled like hay and horses and leather.

"Why did your town wash away? Can you tell me?"

Mae Dean nodded. "It was on low land and the rain flooded it."

"Yes. And where were we when the storm came up before we came up the caprock?"

"Low land," Mae Dean said, beginning to understand.

"That's right. And that's why we had to get to high ground fast. A rain can turn into a flood in a hurry. I didn't want my family to wash away."

Mae Dean caught her breath in a dry sob. "We didn't have to come here," she said softly. "We had a good place to live."

"Yes, we did," Papa answered. "But we didn't have our own land. Land means more than almost anything. This land will take care of us forever. We'll find some higher ground for your play town."

The prairie was green in the soft morning light. The great sky and low horizon seemed to put the whole world at their feet.

"Some day you and your brothers will help build a real town on this prairie," Papa said. "I have a vision of that town. If you try, you can imagine it, too."

Mae Dean looked into the distance. Against the sky, she could almost see a town. Nearby, a prairie dog called.

Mae Dean and Papa turned back toward their dugout. As they walked, Mae Dean sang softly. Papa joined in. "Home, home on the range...."

Home On The Range

Traditional

1. Oh give me a home where the buf - fa - lo roam, where the deer and the an - te - lope play__ where
2. Oh give me a land, where the bright dia - mond sand, flows__ lei - sure - ly down the clear stream,__ where the
3. Oh I would not ex - change, my__ home on the range, where the deer and the an - te - lope play,__ where

sel - dom is heard a dis - cour - ag - ing word, and the skies are not cloud - y all day.
grace - ful white swan, goes__ glid - ing a - long, like a maid in a heav - en - ly dream.
sel - dom is heard, a dis - cour - ag - ing word, and the skies are not cloud - y all day.

Chorus

Home, home on the range,__ where the deer and the an - te - lope play,__ where

sel - dom is heard, a dis - cour - ag - ing word, and the skies are not cloud - y all day.__